Padma Shri Pran

Maurice Horn, the editor of World Encyclopedia of Comics, has described cartoonist PRAN as Walt Disney of India.

Entertaining generation after generation, his comics have been constant companion of all the growing youngsters providing fun and amusement through his famous characters like CHACHA CHAUDHARY, SABU, SHRIMATIJI, PINKI, BILLOO, RAMAN etc. More than 600 of his titles are selling well in the market, and numerous comic strips are regularly appearing in various newspapers. His CHACHA CHAUDHARY comics had already been adapted for a TV Serial, and ran continuously for 600 episodes on a premier channel.

Travelling widely over the globe, he delivers lectures at various International Conferences. He has also been honoured with 'People of The Year Award' by Limca Book of Records for popularizing comics. His comic book 'United We Stand' was released in 1983 by the then Prime Minister Mrs. Indira Gandhi, and is still very popular among children.

Publisher

OUCH !
THUD !

KILL !
KILL !!

AAAAAAAA !

OUCHCHCH !
BANG !

.....7....8....9....10....
BHALU HAS WON THE CHAMPION'S TITLE.

BHALU !
BHALU !!
CHAMP !

IS THERE ANYONE WHO CAN CHALLENGE ME ?

THE LEAF THAT FLIES HIGH, FALLS DOWN SOON.
WHO SPOKE ?

HE SAID THIS.
I'LL TACKLE HIM.

PIGMY ! NOW YOU HAVE TO FIGHT WITH ME.
?

MY PUPIL SABU WILL FIGHT WITH YOU.

I HAVE NO OBJECTION IF HE WANTS TO GET KILLED BY ME.

CRACKK k !
AHH !

BANG !
OHHH !
FIRST ROUND GOES IN BHALU'S FAVOUR.

EVEN IF WE'RE OPPONENTS, YOU ARE A TERRIFIC FIGHTER. BOW DOWN, I WANT TO GIVE MY BLESSINGS.

SEE THE NAILS UNDER HIS WIG. THEY MAKE HIS OPPONENT BLEED WHEN HE BANGS AGAINST HIM.

WHEN SABU IS ANGRY, A VOLCANO BLASTS SOMEWHERE.

HU-HUBA !
SABU !
SABU !!

GO !
AAA-AAA-AAA-

HE WON !

HOW DID YOU REALIZE THAT BHALU IS CHEATING?
BANGING OF THE HEAD GIVES ONE WOUND. BUT SABU GOT MANY WOUNDS. THAT MADE ME SUSPICIOUS.
CHACHA CHAUDHARY'S BRAIN RUNS FASTER THAN A COMPUTER.

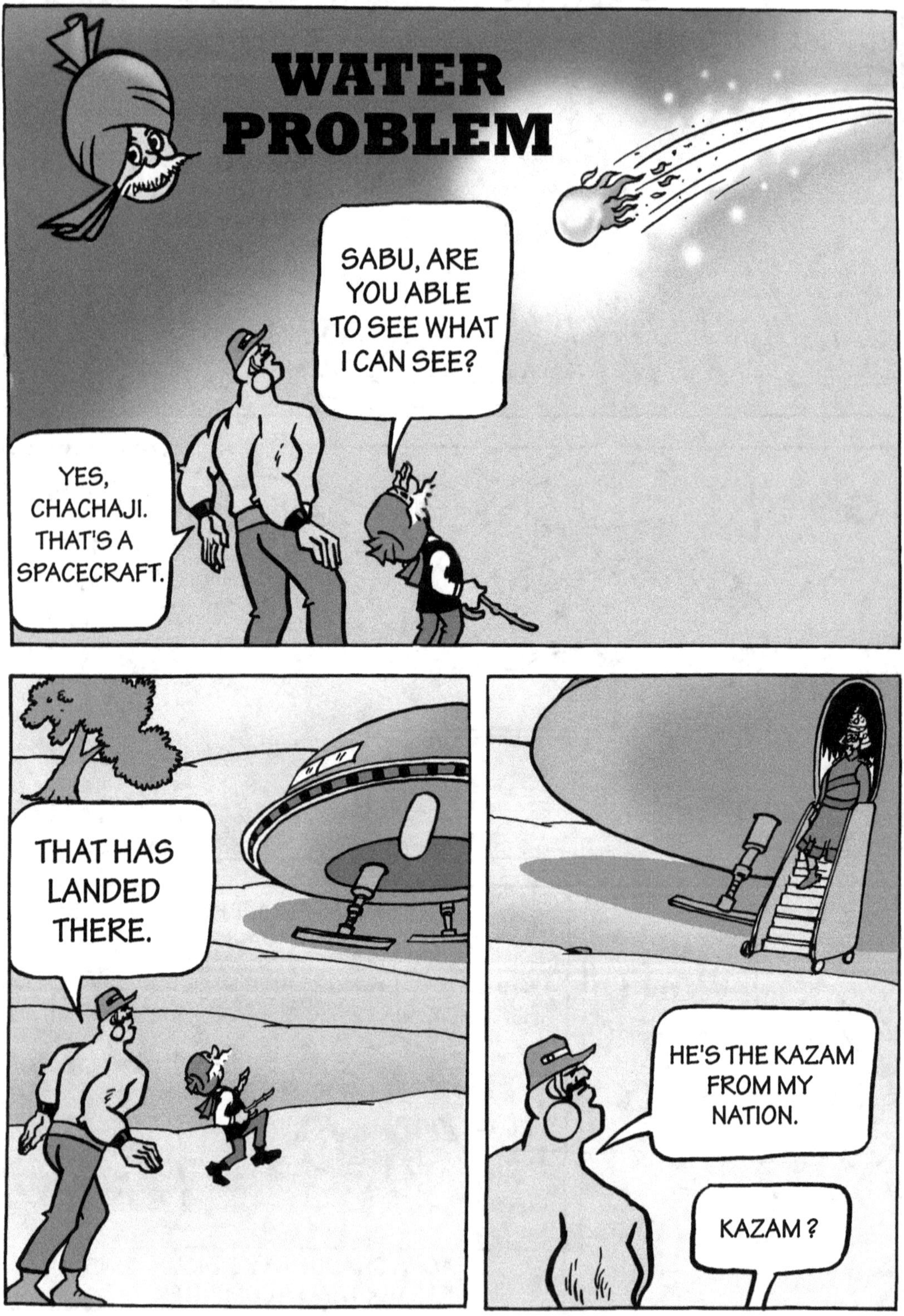

WATER PROBLEM

KAZAM MEANS – GOVERNOR.
HE MUST HAVE COME FOR SOMETHING IMPORTANT.

HOLA !
HOLA !

I SHOULD SWITCH ON THE LANGUAGE SWITCH TO TALK TO THE NATIVES OF EARTH.

WILL YOU HAVE BREAKFAST?
THIS TABLET CONTAINS EVERYTHING- BREAKFAST, LUNCH, DINNER.

WHERE HAD YOU ALL VANISHED AWAY?
BINI ! WE HAVE A GUEST FROM JUPITER.

9

I'LL BRING FOOD FOR YOU.
I HAVE EATEN. I'M THIRSTY. I WANT WATER.
I'LL GIVE THAT TO YOU.

BRING MORE WATER.

MORE…MORE…

I THINK THAT YOU ARE THIRSTY FOR AGES…

THAT'S WHY I'VE COME TO THE EARTH. IN MY LAND, THE PLANET JUPITER THERE'S A DEARTH OF WATER. PEOPLE AND ANIMALS ARE DYING OF THIRST.

OUR SEARCH HAS FOUND THAT CHACHA CHAUDHARY CAN SAVE US FROM THIS TROUBLE.

I BEG OF YOU TO SAVE THE PEOPLE OF MY PLANET.

COME, WE'LL GO THERE AND FIND A SOLUTION TO THIS PROBLEM.

KAZAM'S SPACECRAFT ENTERS SPACE.

THE SOONER WE REACH THERE WOULD BE BETTER.

WATER SCARCITY HAS CAUSED THE DEATH OF HALF THE NATIVES AND ANIMALS OF JUPITER. REST ARE ON THE VERGE OF DEATH.

WATER! MY CHILD HAS BEEN THIRSTY FOR SO MANY DAYS.

LET'S STROLL AROUND THE CITY TO SEE WHERE WE CAN GET WATER FROM NATURE.

STOP!

THIS CRATER CONTAINS WATER, BUT IN THE FORM OF ICE.

WHEN SABU IS ANGRY, A VOLCANO BLASTS SOMEWHERE.

LAVA IS COMING OUT OF THE MOUNTAIN.

WATER! IT'S A MIRACLE.

THIRSTY PEOPLE ARE COMING OUT OF THEIR HOUSES.
WATER!
WATER!

THANKS CHACHAJI. YOU'VE DONE THE IMPOSSIBLE.
YOU SHOULD THANK SABU FOR TAKING YOUR SLAP.

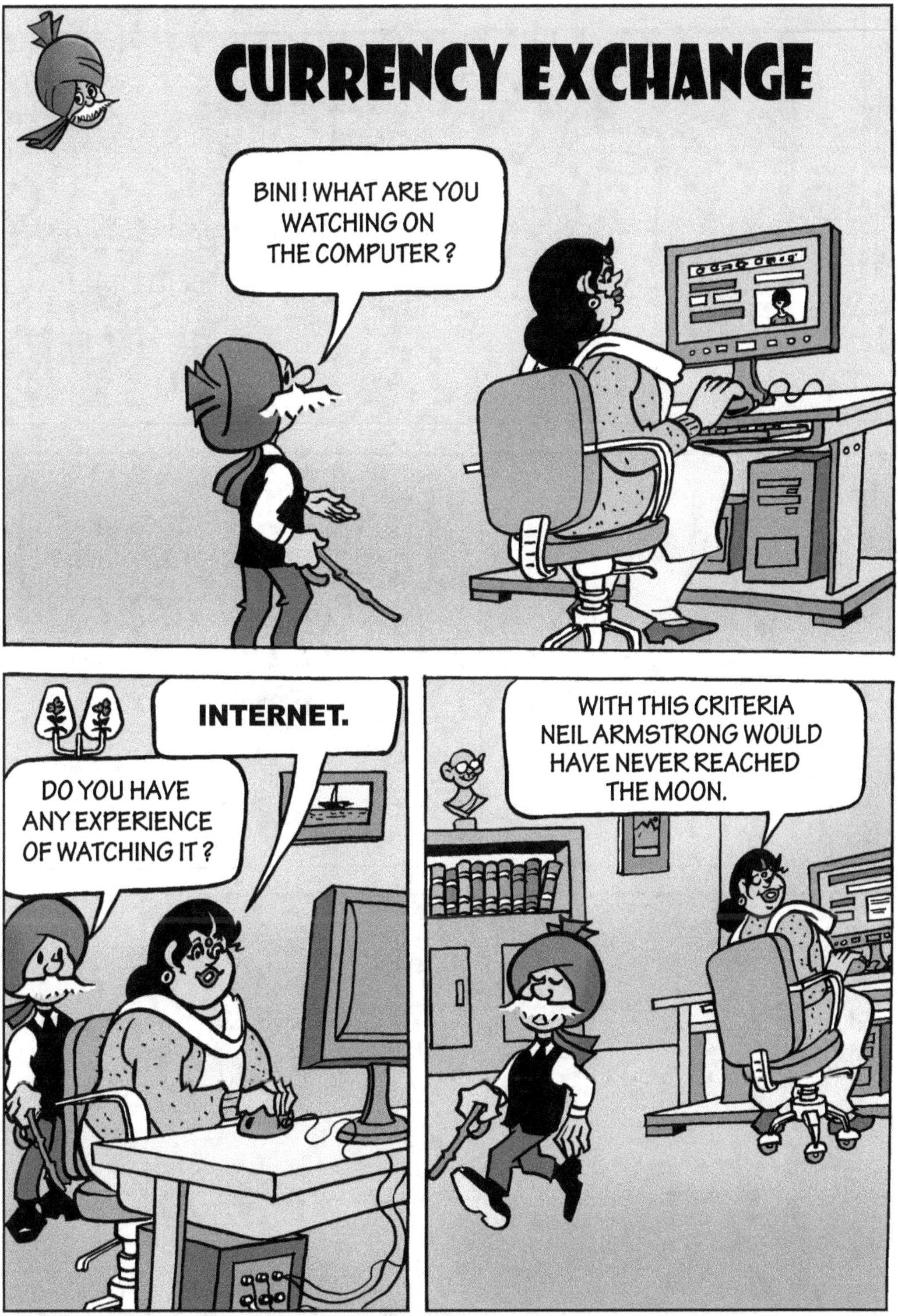

CURRENCY EXCHANGE

LET ME GO AND SEE.

IT'S EMPTY.
MAIL

BINI ! WHAT HAPPENED ?

THE COMPUTER INFORMED THAT THERE IS A MAIL IN THE BOX . I CAME AND SAW THAT IT'S EMPTY.
MAIL

I'LL GO AND TAKE A STROLL.

DABLU ! YOU ARE LOOKING VERY HAPPY.

LOOK OVER THERE ! THAT MAN IS TAKING RS. 1000 AND OFFERING RS. 1500. SEE, HE GAVE ME 3 RS. 500 NOTES.

IT SEEMS TO BE A FISHY THING.

COME, I ALSO WANT TO MEET THAT MAN.
OIL

DRY CLEANERS
CURRENCY EXCHANGE
SEE THERE !

I WANT SOME CURRENCY.
HOW MUCH ?

I WANT IT IN PLACE OF MY GOLD RING.

YOU CAN GET RS. 50,000 FOR THIS.

ACCEPTED.

HERE... RS. 50,000.

BUT YOUR RING IS FAKE.
AND THESE NOTES TOO.

NOW YOU CAN'T GO BACK ALIVE.

CATCH THAT MAN.
CURRENCY EXCHANGE

COME.

BREAKING NEWS – A GANG THAT SMUGGLED FAKE CURRENCY NOTES FROM THE NEIGHBORING COUNTRIES HAS BEEN CAUGHT. THEIR MISSION WAS TO RUIN THE INDIAN ECONOMY.

HOSTAGE

MISS RUBY! HOW MUCH PROFIT HAS OUR COMPANY EARNED THIS YEAR?

SIR, 20000 CRORE AND 65 LAKH RUPEES.
© PRAN'S FEATURES

THIS MEANS THE PUBLIC HAS LIKED OUR PRODUCT.
YES, SIR.

WHO CALLED UP ?

ZUBI SIR, WON'T YOU PAY THE TAX FOR EARNING 20,000 CRORE RUPEES ?

SEND 10,000 CRORE RUPEES. ELSE WE'LL RUIN YOUR ENGINE.

SHUT UP ! A PICKPOCKET LIKE YOU CAN'T SCARE A BIG COMPANY.

MISS RUBY ! INCREASE THE OFFICE SECURITY.

LET'S GO AND MEET THE SETH.

JUBI MUST BE IN HIS OFFICE.

THERE'LL BE SECURITY GUARDS.
LET'S KNOCK THEM FIRST.
ZUBI Ltd

BANG !
OHHH !
CHAIRMAN
www.chachachaudhary.com

SO MR. ZUBI, WHERE'S YOUR SECURITY NOW ?
?!
?!

NOW CALL UP YOUR WIFE AND TELL HER TO BRING 12000 CRORE RUPEES.
BUT YOU HAD ASKED FOR 10000 CRORE RUPEES.
2000 CRORE IS OUR VISITING FEES.

SABU ! SO MUCH EXERCISE WILL MAKE YOU HUNGRIER.

WHO MAKES THE FOOD?
YOU, BINI.
THEN WHY ARE YOU TROUBLED ABOUT SABU'S FOOD?

CHACHA CHAUDHARY! THE GANGSTER BAKAL HAS HELD MY HUSBAND AS HOSTAGE.

BAKAL IS DEMANDING 12000 CRORE RUPEES. OTHERWISE HE'LL KILL THE HOSTAGE.
HE CAN'T DARE TO TOUCH YOUR HUSBAND.

PHARMACY
SWE
YOU GUIDE ME TO BAKAL.

BAKAL! COME AND TAKE YOUR MONEY.
BRING IT HERE.
LET'S GO DOWN.
YOU FOOL! IT'S NOT 12 RUPEES THAT I'LL PUT IN POCKET AND BRING. IT'S A SUM OF 12000 CRORE... AND IT'S LOADED IN THE TRUCK.
ZUB
BAKAL! I HOPE WE'RE NOT BEING TRICKED...
DON'T FORGET, WE STILL HAVE HIM HOSTAGE.

AMOUNT?
OPEN THE TRUCK AND TAKE IT.

COME, LET'S GATHER THE MONEY.

THUD !
OUCH !

INSPECTOR MOZA ! YOU REACHED ON TIME. TAKE GOOD CARE OF THE GUESTS.

INSPECTOR! LET'S GO UPSTAIRS, THERE'S SOMETHING STILL LEFT TO BE DONE.

ARREST THAT GIRL.
??

THANKS FOR HELPING US. BUT WHY ARE YOU ARRESTING MISS RUBY? SHES AN EMPLOYEE IN OUR FIRM.

HOW DID BAKAL COME TO KNOW THAT YOU EARNED A PROFIT OF RS. 20000 CRORE?

SEE THIS. RUBY SENT AN EMAIL TO BAKAL INFORMING ABOUT IT. SHE WAS TO GET A SHARE IN THAT AMOUNT.
CHACHA CHAUDHARY'S BRAIN WORKS FASTER THAN THE COMPUTER.

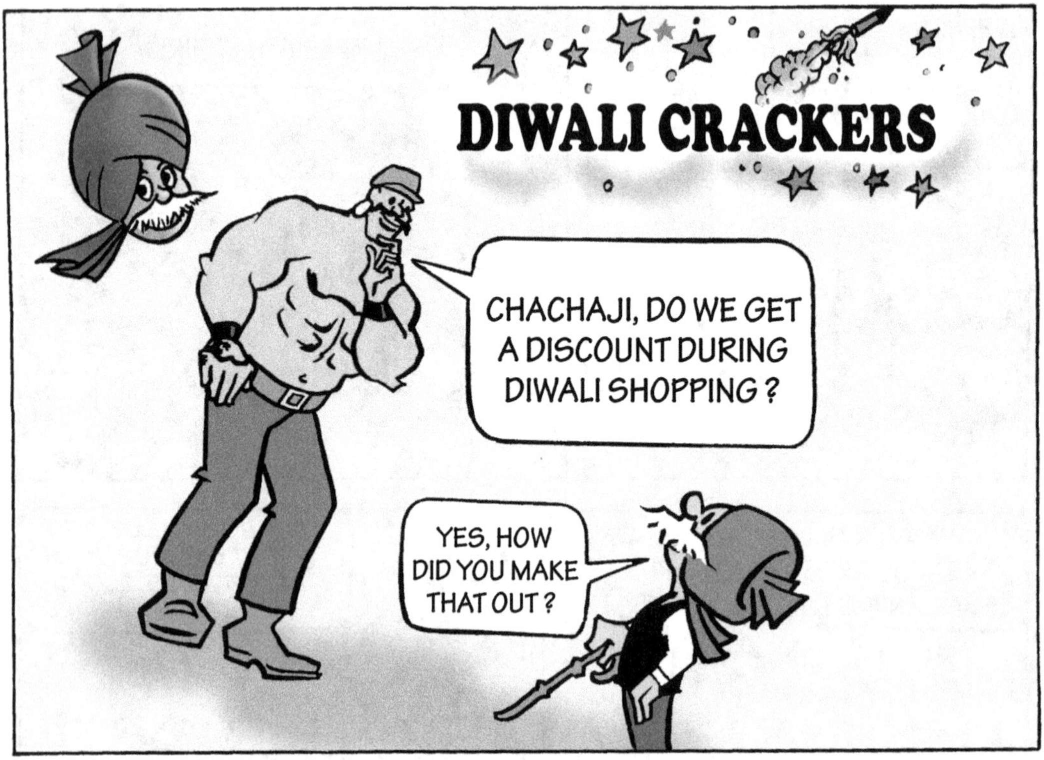

DIWALI CRACKERS

WHAT SHOULD I GIVE TO MY FRIENDS ?

YOU CAN SEND FREE SMS OF GOOD WISHES TO YOUR FRIENDS.

HA ! HA !!

CHACHAJI ! SHOULD WE GET SOME CRACKERS?

BINI ! SABU AND I ARE GOING TO GET CRACKERS.
BRING A POWERFUL BOMB.

BINI ! I CAN'T GET A MORE POWERFUL BOMB THAN YOU.

SABU ! LET'S GO.

AND THEN…
FRIENDS ! THIS IS THE BIGGEST BOMB OF THE WORLD. IT'S RECORDED IN THE GUINNESS BOOK OF WORLD RECORDS AS WELL.
DHAMAKA SINGH ! WHY DON'T YOU PURCHASE THIS BIGGEST BOMB ?

THE HIGHEST BIDDER WILL GET THIS FAMOUS BOMB.
2000 !
5000 !
8000 !

INCREASE THE BID. ELSE WE'LL LOSE IT.

20000 !

WOW ! I GOT THE REAL BIDDER. THE BOMB IS YOURS.

I'LL SELL THIS WONDERFUL BOMB IN 50000 RUPEES.

CRACKERS
THIS IS OUR DESTINATION.

GIVE ME SOME GOOD CRACKERS FOR SABU.
SURE.

SABU! YOU TAKE THE CRACKERS HOME. I'LL BRING THE DRY FRUITS.

AND DON'T BURST ALL BEFORE I RETURN.

STORES
SIR! I REQUIRE GOOD QUALITY DRY FRUIT PACKS.

I'LL GIFT THESE WALNUTS AND ALMONDS TO MY FRIENDS.

EXCHANGING GIFTS MAKES ONE A SOCIAL PERSON.

BATTERY! LET'S SNATCH CHACHAJI'S STUFF.
SCREW! IT'LL BE DONE.

I'LL DISTRACT HIM AND YOU SNATCH HIS BOXES.
OK.

CHACHAJI! AT LEAST BURN ONE ROCKET WITH US.

WHY NOT ?

CHANCE !
www.chachachaudhary.com

SWISHHH !

EXPLODDDDE !
OHHHH !

HAPPY DIWALI !

BINI ! I GOT THE GIFTS FOR MY FRIENDS.

WOW ! THE CRACKERS ARE AMAZING.

DHAMAKA SINGH ?

CHAUDHARY, I'VE COME TO SELL YOU THE BIGGEST CRACKER OF THE WORLD. IT'S EVEN RECORDED IN THE GUINNESS BOOK.

WAIT, I'LL JUST COME OUT.

THIS BOOK DOESN'T MENTION THE CRACKER ANYWHERE.
GUINNESS BOOK

THIS CRACKER IS HOLLOW.

I'VE BEEN CHEATED.

KIDNAPPING

DEAR, CAN I ASK YOU SOMETHING?
HOW BEAUTIFUL AM I?
© PRAN'S FEATURES

JUST LIKE THE EGYPTIAN QUEEN CLEOPATRA.
REALLY?

DO I REALLY LOOK LIKE A QUEEN?
BINI ! DONT YOU TRUST ME?

CAN I MEET CLEOPATRA?

NO ! BECAUSE NOW SHE IS NO LONGER ALIVE.

SO YOU COMPARED ME WITH A DEAD WOMAN?
www.chachachaudhary.com

SHE'S COMING OUT OF THE SCHOOL. KIDNAP HER.
SCHOOL

LEAVE MY HAND. HELPPPP !

HEY, WAIT !

WHAMMM !
OHH !

CATCH THEM! THEY ARE RUNNING AWAY WITH A STUDENT.
SABU! THEY'VE KIDNAPED A STUDENT IN THAT CAR.
TAILORS
CHACHAJI, HOW DID YOU REALIZE THAT THERE'S A STUDENT IN THE CAR?
I SAW THE TIE THAT'S A PART OF THE SCHOOL UNIFORM. SECONDLY, I COULD SEE THE HAND WAVING TO SEEK HELP.
CHACHA CHAUDHARY'S BRAIN RUNS FASTER THAN A COMPUTER.

THEN, LET'S DO SOMETHING.

SOME DISTANCE AWAY...
CHACHAJI, THERE'S THE KIDNAPPER'S VAN. INCREASE THE SPEED.

SABU! GET READY. WE'RE GOING CLOSER TO THEM.

HERE'S OUR CHANCE.

HU- HUBA !

RENGO ! DON'T STOP
THE CAR. KEEP
ON DRIVING.

BANG !!

OUR VAN? HOW
DID THIS HAPPEN?

BECAUSE SABU IS FROM JUPITER, SO HIS BODY IS STRONGER THAN STEEL.

BUT THIS GIRL IS FROM EARTH. I CAN KILL HER.
I DON'T WANT TO DIE.

I'LL GET CRORE OF RUPEES TO RELEASE HER. YOU'VE RUINED OUR CAR. I WANT YOUR TRUCK. ELSE, I AM GOING TO KILL HER.

BEFORE THAT I'LL BANG YOU.
WAIT, SABU!

KILLING THE HOSTAGE WOULD WASTE THE CRORE OF RUPEES THAT YOU CAN GET.

GIVE ME THE TRUCK'S IGNITION KEY.

I WANT TO WARN YOU, DON'T GET INTO TROUBLE.
THIS RED TURBAN MAN IS DISTRACTING US. KILL THE GIRL.
PLEASE, SAVE ME !

HERE, TAKE THE TRUCK KEYS.

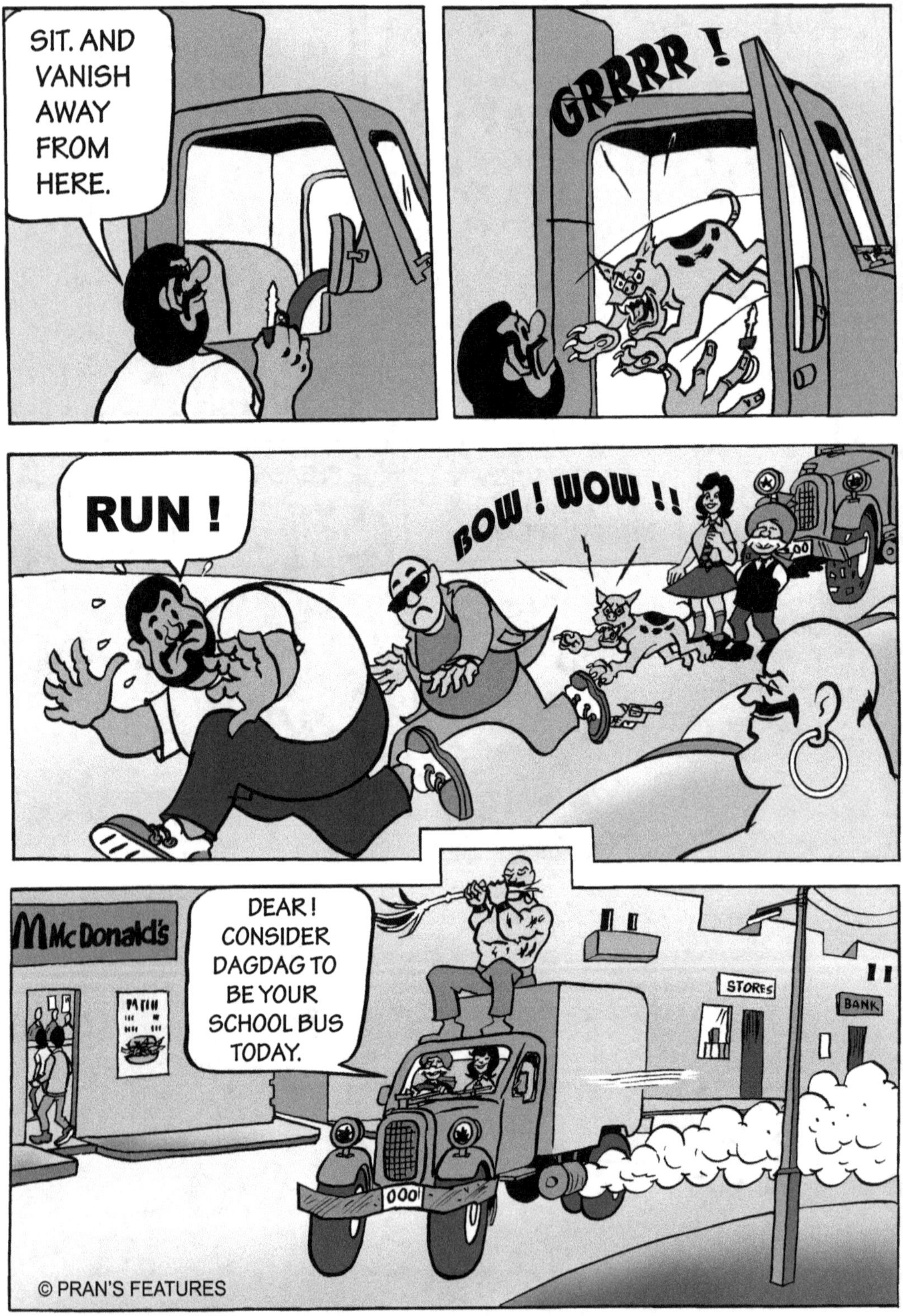

SIT. AND VANISH AWAY FROM HERE.

GRRRR !

RUN !
BOW ! WOW !!

DEAR ! CONSIDER DAGDAG TO BE YOUR SCHOOL BUS TODAY.
McDonald's
PATH
STORES
BANK
0001

PEARLS

SABU! LET'S GO FOR A SWIM.

LET'S GO IN THE WATER.
WHY NOT? IT'LL BE AN AMAZING ADVENTURE.

THEY'RE GOING INTO THE DEPTH OF THE SEA.

IT'S A STRANGE ATMOSPHERE HERE.

AHHH! BEAUTIFUL SHELL!

BINI CAN GET THIS PRECIOUS PEARL STUDDED IN THE RING.

OHHH ! A WHALE IS FOLLOWING ME.

OUCH !! MOTI HAS SLIPPED OUT OF MY HANDS.

AND IT HAS GONE IN THE MOUTH OF THE BIG FISH.

NOW THAT HUGE CREATURE ISN'T FOLLOWING US.

SABU ! IT'S RELEASING THE WATER DUE TO WHICH MANY PRECIOUS PEARLS ARE ALSO COMING OUT WHICH IT MUST HAVE SWALLOWED. CATCH THEM.

AH ! I GATHERED SO MANY. THEY'RE ENOUGH FOR A JEWELLERY SET.

SABU ! HE'S BRINGING PRECIOUS PEARLS.

I'LL HIDE UNDER HIS CHAIR AND STEAL THE PEARLS WHEN HE WILL TAKE REST.
www.chachachaudhary.com

I'LL KEEP THE PEARLS ON THE STOOL AND TAKE REST.

47

THEY'RE SAFE HERE.

NOW I'LL LIE DOWN AND TAKE REST.

CRACK K !
OH ! THE CHAIR BROKE DOWN.
OUCHHH !

CHACHI ! SEE WE BROUGHT REAL PEARLS FOR YOU.
TODAY I'LL GIVE SPECIAL BUTTERMILK TO BOTH OF YOU.

CHACHA CHAUDHARY ™
AND SULTAN

SULTAN JHAJJAR NATH OF SURATGARH.
HIS HIGHNESS ! YOU'VE BECOME OLD. FROM NOW ONWARDS I'LL BE THE KING.
WAZIR KALIKH ! I'M HAVING DOUBT ON YOUR LOYALTY.

SILENCE ! FROM TODAY I'M THE SULTAN !

MY PEOPLE WILL TEACH YOU A LESSON .
NOW YOU ARE NOT A KING, ONLY A SLAVE.

YOU ALL ARE LOYAL TO OLD KING. I'M GOING TO KILL YOU.
MERCY !

DICTATOR KALIKH STARTED KILLING EVERYONE.

WAZIR KHAUF! TAKE AWAY ALL THE LAND FROM THE PEOPLE AND DISTRIBUTE IT AMONG MY RELATIVES.

COLLECT SO MUCH TAX FROM EVERYONE THAT MY SAFE GETS FULL.

OBEY MY ORDERS ! FAST!
AS YOU SAY ! MY LORD.

BABA! WHO CAN STOP KALIKH FROM DOING WRONG?
CHACHA CHAUDHARY! HE'S AN OLD FRIEND OF SULTAN JHAJJAR.

YOUNG SHERA GOES TO MEET CHACHA CHAUDHARY.
RUN BADAL!

CHACHA JI! I'VE COME FROM SURATGARH.
HOW'S MY FRIEND SULTAN JHAJJARNATH?

KALIKH HAS PUT HIM IN JAIL. HE'S KILLING INNOCENT PEOPLE.
WE'LL TRY TO GET PEACE AND HARMONY.

NOW I CAN GO BACK IN PEACE.
COME DUGDUG! SULTAN NEEDS OUR HELP.

ONE BECOMES BLIND WHEN HE GETS POWER.

STOP ! YOU CAN'T GO INSIDE.
WE'VE COME TO CONGRATULATE THE NEW SULTAN.

WELCOME FRIENDS OF KALIKH !

CRUEL KALIKH! RELEASE THE SULTAN. AND BRING PEACE IN YOUR KINGDOM.

FRIENDS OF JHAJJAR ! I'LL GET YOU KILLED BY MY ELEPHANTS.

IINN...
N!
KILL THEM BY TRAMPLING UNDER YOUR FEET.

IINN...
N!
MAD KING'S... MAD ELEPHANT!

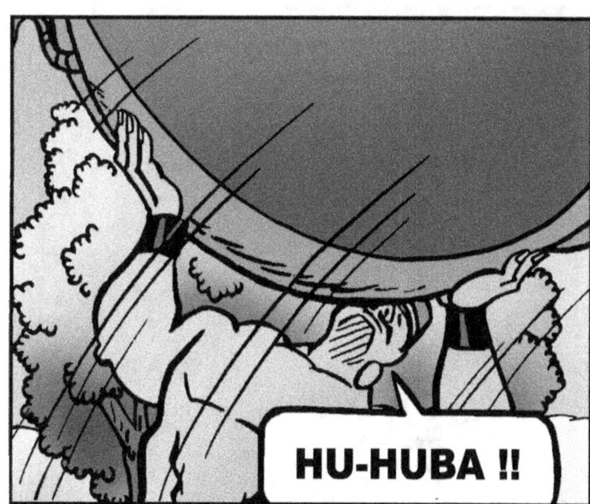

HU-HUBA !!

SWOOSH H !
THERE YOU GO!

GO SABU ! AND GET JHAJJARNATH RELEASED FROM JAIL.

SULTAN MUST BE PRISONED HERE. I'LL BREAK THIS CEILING.

CHACHA CHAUDHARY! EVEN SABU CANNOT SAVE THE SULTAN FROM BEING KILLED.
CRACK K !

YOU CAN'T TOUCH HIM TILL I'M ALIVE.

PLEASE HELP ME. TAKE ME DOWN.

YOU GO WHERE YOU SHOULD BE.
SWOOSH H !

WHAM M !

IT'S AN END OF THE DICTATORSHIP.

JHAJJARNATH RETURNS TO POWER.
CHACHA JI ! COME AND STAY WITH ME FOR A FEW DAYS.
NOW I MUST TAKE A LEAVE.

COME ! THERE ARE MORE SERIOUS ISSUES TO BE SOLVED.

IT'S BEEN A LONG TIME YOURS CHACHI HAS COOKED FOOD FOR US.

CHACHI ! IT'LL BE GREAT IF YOU CAN COOK SOME FOOD FOR US.
WHY ! YOUR FRIEND SULTAN DIDN'T OFFER CHAPPAN BHOG TO EAT !

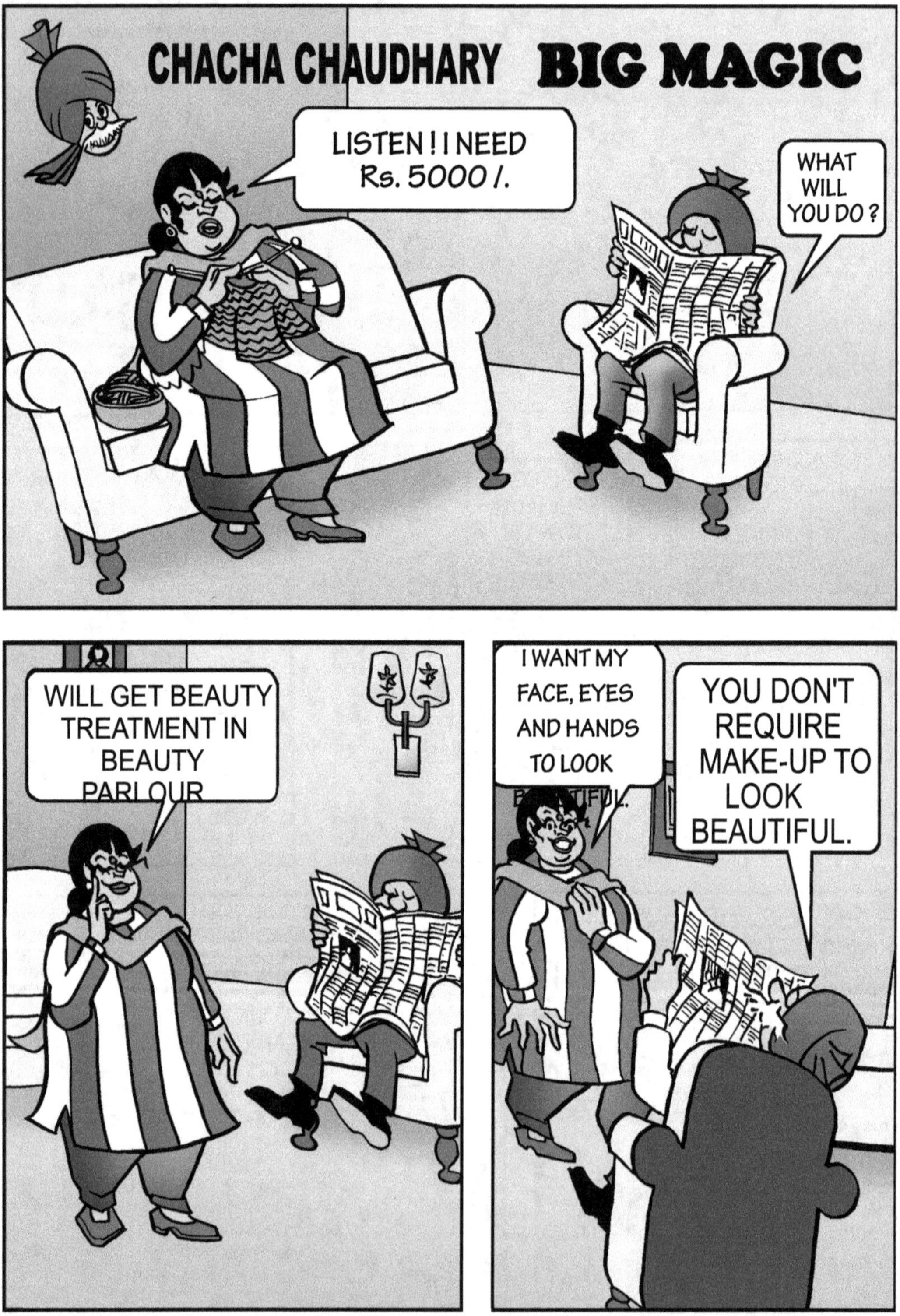

CHACHA CHAUDHARY BIG MAGIC

SMILE … YOU'LL LOOK MORE BEAUTIFUL.
WHAT SHALL I DO TO LOOK MORE ATTRACTIVE ?

SPEAK WELL. PEOPLE WILL GET ATTRACTED BY WHAT YOU SPEAK.

WHAT ABOUT MY HANDS ?
YOU SHOULD DONATE WITH YOUR HANDS TO THE POOR.

WHAT A FOOL I AM ! THE PERSON WHOSE BRAIN WORKS FASTER THAN THE COMPUTER …

ALWAYS FINDS EXCUSES FOR NOT GIVING ME MONEY.
I SHOULD GET OUT OF HERE. ELSE BINNI WILL DISTURB MY MAKE-UP.

FRIENDS! I'VE DECIDED THAT TODAY WE'LL FINISH CHACHA CHAUDHARY.
THAT'S A BRILLIANT IDEA! CHIEF DHAMAKA SINGH !

WE'LL CELEBRATE AFTER COMPLETING THE MISSION.

THAT RED TURBAN IS A DANGER FOR OUR UNDERWORLD.

HERE IS HIS HOME .

I'LL FINISH HIM ! COME !
WAIT ! LET ME DO THAT.

LET ME FINISH HIM WITHOUT GIVING HIM A CHANCE.
RAT-TATT !

CHIMTE ! THE WORK IS DONE. LET'S GO.

AND I'LL BE CALLED.. SUPER DON!!
BY KILLING CHACHA YOU'LL GET GREAT RESPECT IN THE CRIME WORLD.
DLH 111

FRINEDS ! I'VE FINISHED OUR ENEMY.

FROM TODAY I'M THE KING OF THE CRIME WORLD, SUPER DON DHAMAKA SINGH!
CONGRATS !

LET'S CELEBRATE. GET LADOOS FOR EVERYBODY.

NOT LADOOS… RASGULLA!! I LIKE RASGULLAS.

HOW ARE YOU ALIVE ? IS IT A MAGIC ?

YES ! IT'S CALLED CHACHA CHAUDHARY'S BIG MAGIC !

THE PERSON ON WHOM YOU SPRAYED BULLETS WAS A TOY.

ONE TOY COMPANY HAS MANUFACTURED TOYS LIKE ME FOR THE KIDS.

IT WAS ONLY A TOY ON WHOM YOU SHOT AT.
I MADE A TERRIBLE MISTAKE.

BOSS!! THAT WAS A TOY. BUT HE'S REAL. LET'S SHOOT HIM HERE.

CHACHA JI! YOU'VE SPOKEN ENOUGH. NOW MY GUN WILL SPEAK.

THUDD!
I KNOW HOW TO DEAL WITH YOU GUYS.

HOW DARE YOU TO ATTACK OUR CHIEF !
RAT-TAT-T-T !
GOOD !

KADDU ! I'LL SQUEEZE YOU !
KARA-BOOM MM !
WHEN SABU GETS ANGRY SOMEWHERE VOLCANO ERRUPTS !

RUN ! FOR OUR LIVES !
HEY ! DON'T LEAVE ME LIKE THIS.

FOR YOU I'M ENOUGH. A ONE MAN ARMY !
RAT-TAT-T-T !
HEY ! OLD GRAMOPHONE RECOR ! YOU'VE SUNG ENOUGH NOW !!

GET OUT OF HERE !!
WHAMM !

LEAVE THIS CRIME WORLD. WORK HARD AND START EARNING IN A TOY FACTORY.

BEST FRIEND

CHACHA JI ! HOW MANY FRIENDS DO YOU HAVE ?
EVERYONE IS MY FRIEND.
BINNI IS ALSO MY FRIEND.

SO IS ROCKET .

ALL THE GREEN TREES, COLOURFUL FLOWERS AND BUTTERFLIES... ALL ARE MY FRIENDS.

BUT WHO IS YOUR BEST FRIEND ?

THERE ARE TWO PEOPLE WHOM I CAN'T OFFEND !
WHO ARE THEY ?

ONE IS GOD ! OTHER IS MY DOCTOR ! IF GOD GETS ANGRY, HE SENDS US TO A DOCTOR.

IF DOCTOR CAN'T CURE US, WE GO TO GOD FOR OUR LIVES.

HA ! HA ! CHACHA JI. YOU'VE GOT VERY DEEP THOUGHTS.

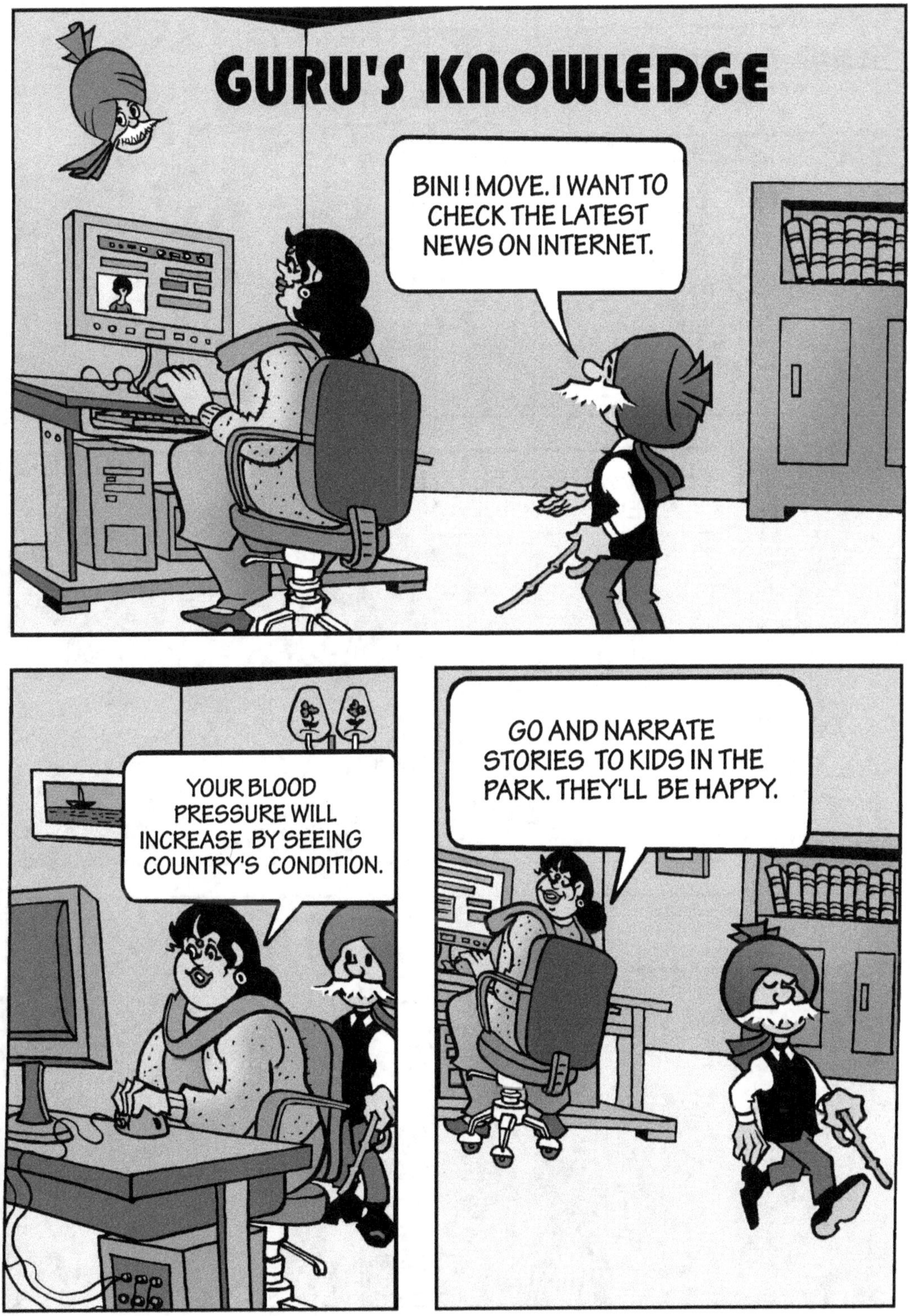

GURU'S KNOWLEDGE

I WANT TO DO SHOPPING ON THE NET.

ROCKET! THANK YOUR STARS THAT YOU ARE NOT MARRIED.

CHACHA JI! PLEASE TELL US A NEW STORY TODAY!
SURE !

KIDS! WHAT WOULD YOU LIKE TO LISTEN ? A STORY OR A JOKE ?
CHACHAJI! I WANT TO ASK YOU SOMETHING.

PLEASE GO AHEAD.

YOU ALWAYS TELL HUMOROUS INCIDENTS TO US. FROM WHERE DO YOU GET ALL THESE ?

MY SCHOOL TEACHER USED TO TELL , THOSE WHOM MAKE OTHERS LAUGH GO TO HEAVEN.

I FOLLOW HIS THINKING AND SHARE LOVE AND LAUGHTER EVERYWHERE.

GREAT ! YOUR TEACHER MUST HAVE BEEN VERY INTELLIGENT.

ONLY YOUR GURU GIVES YOU THE REAL KNOWLEDGE. GO AND PLAY NOW. SO, YOU'LL HAVE A GOOD BODY ANDTHEN MIND WILL WORK FAST.
HURRAY! CHACHA JI YOU ARE THE BEST.

PRINCESS

WOW ! MUSCLEMAN.
TODAY YOU ARE
EXERCISING !

BOXING
MAKES
ME STRONG
AND ALERT.

EXERCISE
MAKES ME
HUNGRY
ALSO.

FOOD
IS
READY.

GREAT ! HAVING THESE
PARANTHAS AND COLD
LASSI FROM CHACHI JI !

DRIVER! STOP THE CAR. CHACHA JI'S HOUSE HAS COME.

GOOD MORNING, CHACHA JI. I'M THE PRINCESS OF DIBRUGARH, DONA!
TELL ME HOW CAN I HELP YOU?

I'VE STARTED LIKING SABU.

I WANT TO MARRY HIM.
BUT HE IS HAPPY BEING SINGLE. AND WANTS TO REMAIN LIKE THAT.

I DON'T THINK HE WILL REFUSE MY PROPOSAL.
WHY HAS THIS PRINCESS COME HERE TO DISTURB ME!

?!
SABU ! IF WE GET MARRIED, OUR KIDS WILL BE BEAUTIFUL LIKE ME AND STRONG LIKE YOU.
OH ! SHE HAS COME PREPARED WITH FUTURE PLANNING !

SABU, YOU SHOULD ACCEPT HER PROPOSAL. SHE'S BEAUTIFUL AND INTELLIGENT TOO.

CHACHA JI ! I CAN'T REFUSE YOU. I'LL MARRY HER BUT ...?

EVERYONE KNOWS ABOUT MY DIET. I'LL MARRY THAT GIRL WHO CAN COOK WELL.

I DON'T WANT THAT AFTER MARRIAGE CHACHI SHOULD COOK FOR ME.

WOW ! YOU ARE SO CONSIDERATE !

BUT AT OUR PLACE, CHIEF PREPARES THE FOOD.

DONA ! I PREFER EATING HOME COOKED FOOD FROM MY WIFE'S HAND.

ONE HAS TO SACRIFICE IN LOVE AND WAR.

MY DEAR ! I'LL LEARN COOKING FOR YOU. NOW YOU ACCEPT MY PROPOSAL.

PRINCESS ! IT'S EASY TO SAY THAN DO.
I'M A STUBURN GIRL. MY WORDS ARE FINAL.

DONA. SABU HAS THIRTY PARANTHAS AT ONE TIME ALONG WITH VEGETABLES, DAAL AND LASSI.

OH ! IT'S TOO MUCH OF HARD WORK.

HALF OF MY LIFE WILL BE SPENT IN THE KITCHEN.

CHACHA JI ! WHY HAS SHE GONE BACK?
COOKING EVERYDAY FOR YOU WOULD HAVE SPOILT HER FANCY NAIL ART DESIGN !

VEGETARIAN

SWOOSH H !
THUD D !
OH !

PONGA UNCLE ! PLEASE RETURN OUR BALL.
GET LOST FROM HERE.

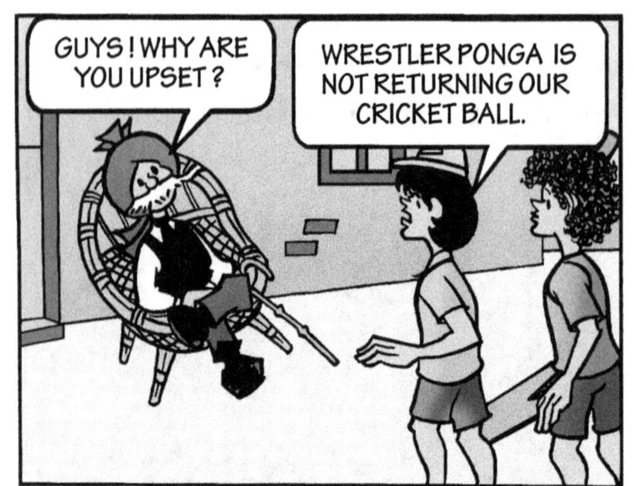

GUYS! WHY ARE YOU UPSET?
WRESTLER PONGA IS NOT RETURNING OUR CRICKET BALL.

COME! LET ME SOLVE YOUR PROBLEM.

THIS CHACHAJI CONCERNED ABOUT EVERYONE EXCEPT HIS FAMILY.

I'M A SOCIAL WORKER SINCE MY CHILDHOOD.

HE HAS TAKEN OUR BALL AND CLOSED THE DOOR.
HE'LL RETURN THE BALL. YOU WAIT AND WATCH.

DING! BONG!!
OPEN THE DOOR, PONGA SAHIB!

WELCOME ! CHACHA JI.

PLEASE SIT DOWN.

PLEASE HAVE SOME DELICIOUS RICE PULAV.
THANKS ! I JUST HAD LUNCH.

OH NO ! CHACHA JI IS HAVING LUNCH.
HAVE PATIENCE. LET'S SEE WHAT WILL HAPPEN.

I REMEMBER THAT YOU A ARE PURE VEGETARIAN !

GORGE BERNAD SHAW HAS SAID OUR STOMACH IS NOT A GRAVEYARD FOR DEAD ANIMALS. I'M VERY MUCH IMPRESSED BY HIS PHILOSOPHY.
GREAT !

I'LL KEEP THE RICE PLATE AND COME.

SOME TIME BACK A CRICKET BALL HAD COME HERE.
I'LL NOT RETURN IT.

CAN I SEE IT ?
I'LL GET IT. BUT WHAT'S THERE TO SEE IN IT?

ARE YOU PURE VEGETARIAN?
SURE !! I'VE NEVER EVEN TOUCHED NON VEG IN MY LIFE.

CHACHA CHAUDHARY HAS STARTED TALKING ABOUT VEGETARIAN AND NON VEG.
WE HAD COME FOR SOMETHING ELSE... OUR BALL.

THIS IS A LEATHER BALL !!
SO WHAT !

THIS LEATHER BALL IS MADE FROM THE SKIN OF A DEAD ANIMAL.
OHH ! I NEVER THOUGHT ABOUT IT.

KEEP THIS LEATHER BALL AWAY FROM MY HOUSE.
?!

YOU SHOULD PLAY WITH A RUBBER BALL.

MONTU ! HE HAS RETURNED OUR BALL.

CHACHA CHAUDHARY YOU ARE GREAT !
GUYS ! GO AND PLAY IN A PLAYGROUND , NOT IN THE STREET.

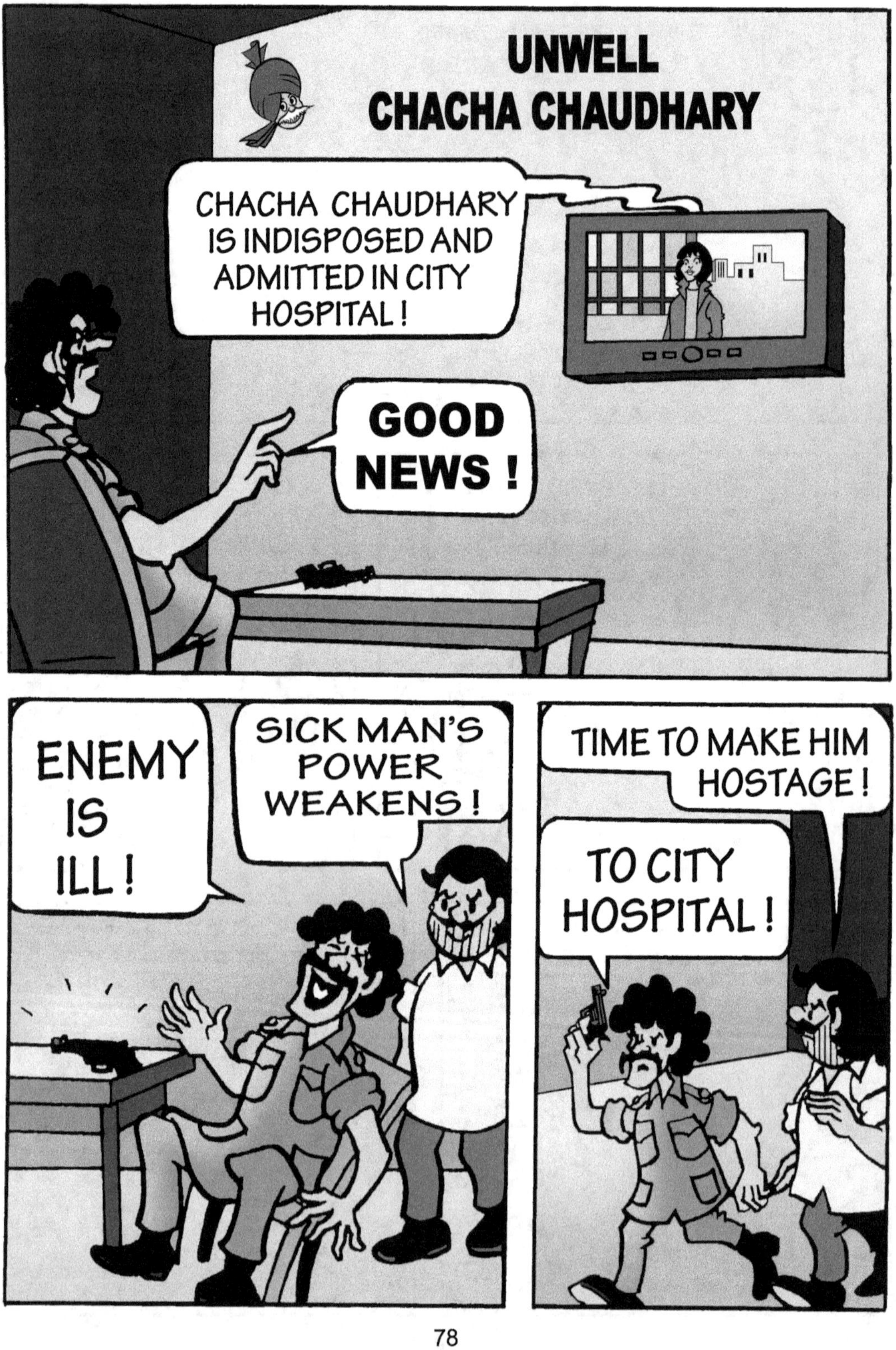

UNWELL CHACHA CHAUDHARY

TODAY HE'LL FACE DEFEAT!

IF WE SUCCEED, ALL UNDERWORLD WOULD ACCEPT ME AS THEIR SUPREME COMMANDER!

WE'LL CELEBERATE THE EVENT!
THAT WOULD BE THE HAPPIEST DAY FOR THE OUTLAWS!

BOSS! WE HAVE REACHED THE HOSPITAL!

WE'LL OVERPOWER HIM UNWARE!
CITY HOSPITAL

??
DOCTOR! IN WHICH ROOM IS CHAUDHARY?

THERE!
I.C.U

HURRY!
WE SHOULD NOT GIVE HIM CHANCE TO ESCAPE!

HANDS UP!

CHACHA JI! YOUR PLAN TO APPREHEND DHAMAKA SINGH SUCCEEDED WELL!
POLICE

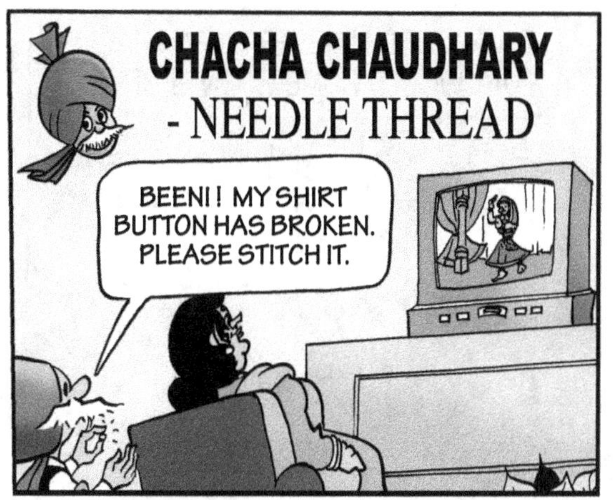

CHACHA CHAUDHARY
- NEEDLE THREAD
BEENI! MY SHIRT BUTTON HAS BROKEN. PLEASE STITCH IT.

I CAN'T FIND A NEEDLE. YOU BRING A NEEDLE, I'LL MEND IT.

LET ME STITCH THE TORN PART.

THAT BEGGAR HAS A NEEDLE.

SHOES
TV
WILL YOU LEND ME YOUR NEEDLE?

OH MY GOD ! I NEVER KNEW THAT A DAY WOULD COME WHEN PEOPLE WILL BEG FROM BEGGARS.

I'LL TRY MY LUCK SOMEWHERE ELSE.

CHACHAJI ! WHERE ARE YOU RUNNING OFF TO?
© PRAN'S FEATURES

BILLOO ! I AM SEARCHING FOR A NEEDLE.

WAIT ! I'LL GET IT FROM INSIDE.

TAKE IT !

SILLY ! THIS ISN'T A NEEDLE, IT'S A PIN.

FORGET THE NEEDLE. I'LL TAKE A NEW SHIRT.
BUY 5 GET 5 FREE.

I LIKE THIS ONE.
YOU WEAR IT AND SEE.

SIR, MONEY?
YOU'VE WRITTEN ON THE BOARD-BUY 1 GET 1 FREE. SO, I'VE TAKEN THE FREE ONE.

BALAAKA

SABU ! SAVE YOURSELF !

WHY DID YOU WANT TO HIT SABU? WHAT HARM HAVE WE CAUSED YOU ?

I AM BALAAKA- UNCLE OF RAKA ! YOU HAVE TROUBLED MY NEPHEW MUCH ! ! I CHAVE COME FOR REVENGE !

SABU! SUPER FAST BOWLING!
WHAM M!
I'LL NOT REST UNTIL I HAVE KILLED YOU!

WHAM M!
AAOWWW!

HOW DARE YOU?

BANG G!

MY GUN!
NOW NO ONE CAN RETRIEVE IT!

STOP ARMS RACE !
CRACK!

YOU BROKE MY GUN ? I'LL BREAK YOUR MOUTH !

WHAM M!

MY FINGERS BROKE !
SABU IS THE INHABITANT OF JUPITER ! THEREFORE HIS BONES ARE STRONGER THAN STEEL !

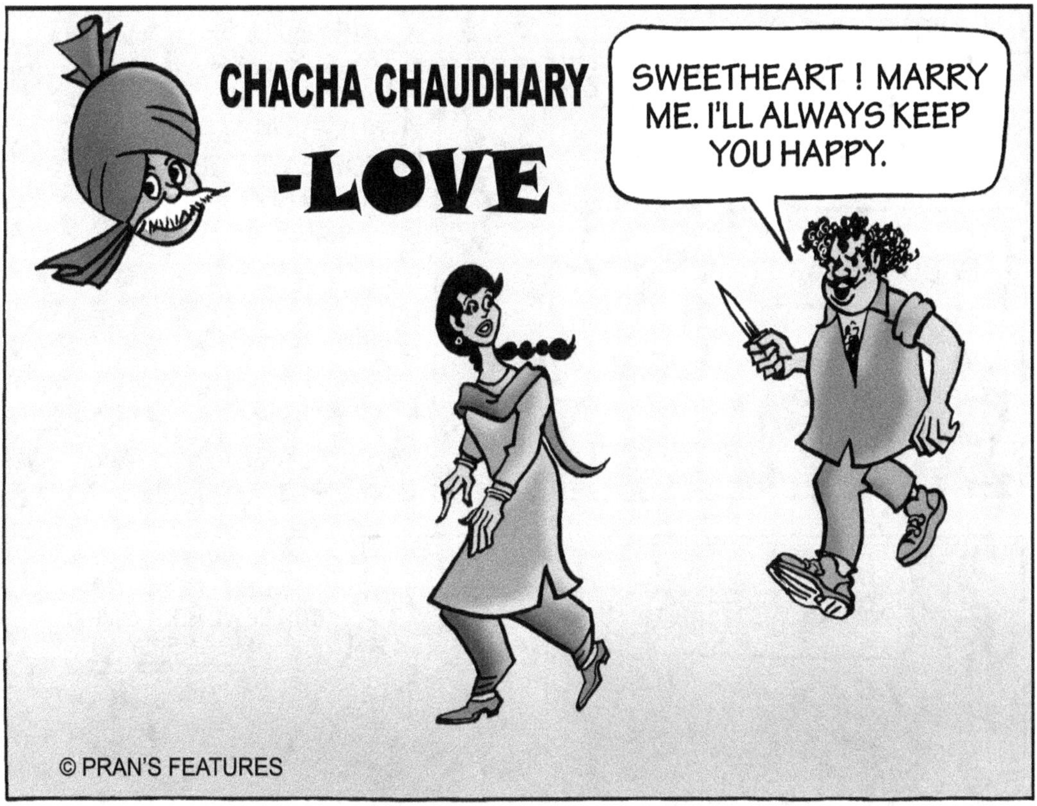

CHACHA CHAUDHARY

-LOVE

WHERE IS HE WHO TEASES GIRLS? I'LL BREAK HIS BONES.
SABU, RELAX !

IF YOU'LL BE ANGRY, THEN A VOLCANO WILL BURST OUT AND PEOPLE WILL GET HOMELESS. I'LL TACKLE THIS PROBLEM.

YOU DO AS I SAY...

NEXT DAY...
AHA, SWEETHEART ! I WON'T LET YOU GO TODAY WITHOUT GIVING ME A REPLY.

RULDOO, LOOK AT THE GIRL THERE. SHE'S PRETTIER THAN ME. WHY DON'T YOU MARRY HER?
WOW !

REALLY... VERY PRETTY.
DARLING, I WANT TO MARRY YOU.

LOOK AT THAT GIRL, SHE'S A FILM ACTRESS. YOU'LL BE BENEFITTED IF YOU MARRY HER.

WOW !
HOW LOVELY FEET !

WHY DO YOU TEASE GIRLS?
BUT SHE SAID THAT YOU ARE AN ACTRESS.

I DO STUNTS IN THE MOVIES.
THUDD !

TIT FOR TAT

SIR! SAY SOME EXPERIENCE OF ARMY?

ONCE I WAS GIVING TRAINING TO NEW RECRUITS.

I NOTICED THAT ONE OF THEM MIGHT BE AN EX-CRIMINAL.

I SAW, EVERY TIME THAT PARTICULAR SEPOY FIRES, HE CLEANED AND REMOVED HIS FINGER PRINTS FROM GUN. THAT CONFIRMED MY SUSPICION!

TRUE!
© PRAN'S FEATURES

CHAUDHARY! NOW IT IS YOUR TURN.

ONCE A DICTATOR ORDERED TO PRINT HIS PHOTO ON EVERY STAMP.

AFTER FEW DAYS SECRETARY BROUGHT AND SHOWED POSTAGE STAMPS TO DICTATOR. BUT HE COULD NOT HIS PHOTO.

WHERE IS MY PHOTO? DICTATOR ROARED.

SECRETARY TURNED STAMP AND SHOWED DICTATOR'S PHOTO PHOTO PRINTED ON THE SIDE OF STAMP WHERE PEOPLE APPLY SPITTLE.

HA! HA!!

LET ME LEAVE. BINI'S HAS WAITING FOR ME!

Enter the door 1. Get out of the maze through the door 2. Closed doors are locked. Good luck to you !

ANEMONE
COD
CORAL REEF
CRAB
DOLPHIN
FISH
FLYING FISH
HALIBUT
HERRING
JELLYFISH
LOBSTER
MORAY EEL
MUSSEL
OCEAN
OCTOPUS

OYSTER
PLANKTON
SALMON
SCUBA DIVING
SEABED
SEAHORSE
SEAWEED
SHARK
SHELL
SQUID
STARFISH
STINGRAY
TURTLE
URCHIN
WHALE

★★★★☆

____ X ROT

RA X ____

CAB X ____ X E

ZUC X ____ X I

TO X ____ X O

S X ____ X ACH

O X ____

P X ____

MU X ____ X D

____ X KIN

PI X ____ X PLE

Fill in the blanks with the words BAG, CAR, CHIN, DISH, EAR, KIN, MAT, NEAP, PIN, PUMP, RANGE, STAR to reveal the names of 11 edible plants (mostly fruits and vegetables).

Find the seven
differences between
the two pictures.

Celebrating !ndia

get inspired by great personalities of India

The Great Indian Biography Series

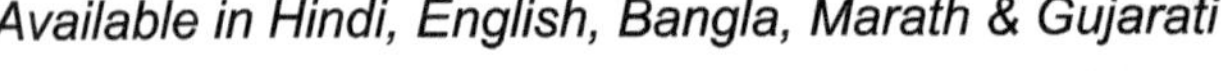

Available in Hindi, English, Bangla, Marath & Gujarati

Order Now